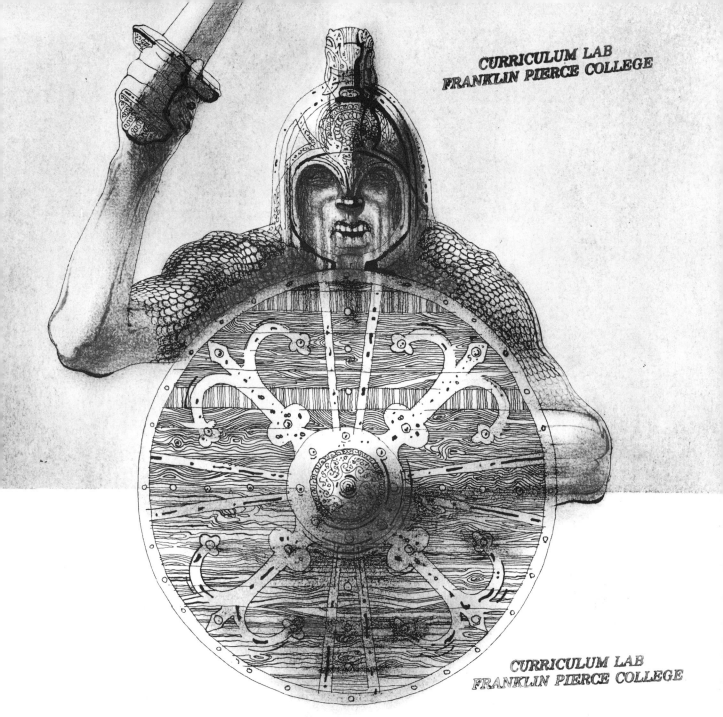

BEOWULF

CHARLES KEEPING
KEVIN CROSSLEY-HOLLAND

Oxford University Press

OXFORD TORONTO MELBOURNE

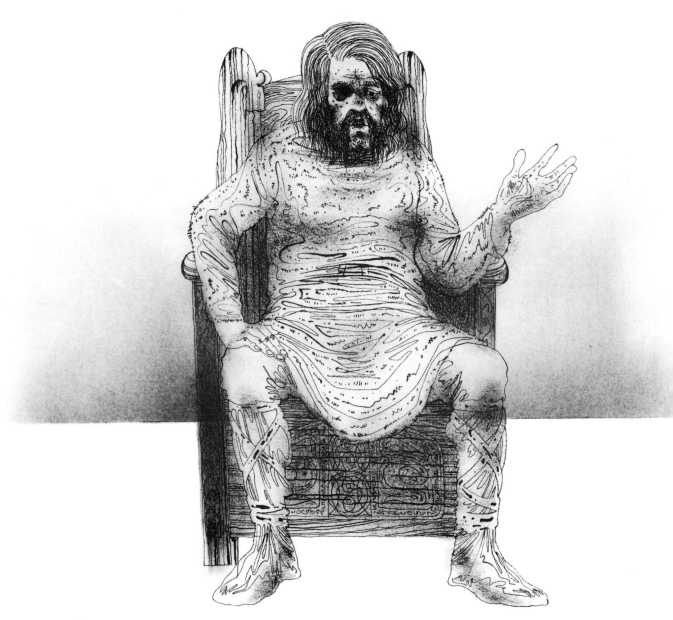

S TRANGER!' called Hygelac.
The men near the king stopped talking and picking their teeth and swilling stonecold mead over their gums.

'Stranger!' called Hygelac.

In the hall of the king of the Geats, a hundred men listened. Almost silence. The cat-fire hissed and spat, golden-eyed tapestries winked out of the gloom. Silence. The man rose from the stranger's seat.

'Your name?' demanded Hygelac.

'Gangleri,' said the stranger. 'In your tongue: Wanderer.'

'All right, Wanderer. It's time you sang for your supper.'

Men on the mead-benches shifted their buttocks, and stretched out their legs. The gathering faced inwards towards the fire.

Wanderer stood in the poet's place by the hearth and rubbed his one gleaming eye. 'I'll fuel you,' he said, 'with a true story, and one close to my heart. This story of past and present and future.'

'True?' called out a young man, the king's nephew, Beowulf by name. 'How can it be true if it's in the future?'

'Because it is not finished,' said Wanderer. 'You must finish it.'

Beowulf, how old was he, not more than twenty, felt his cheeks flush with quickening blood.

Wanderer stooped and scooped up six-stringer, the harp that always stood in the poet's place. Gleaming maplewood, white willow pegs, white fingertips, a quivering face.

'Listen!' said Wanderer. 'A story of heroes!' Now he plucked the harp with a plectrum. 'A story of monsters!' And plucked it again. 'A story of Denmark!'

'Ugh!' said Hygelac, and spat into the straw at his feet. 'The old enemy.'

But Beowulf leaned forward. Hadn't his own father Ecgtheow once taken refuge with the Danes? Hadn't Hrothgar, the Danish king, saved his father's skin? Hrothgar ... he sounded a good man.

'The first king of the Danes was Scyld Scefing,' said Wanderer. 'I loved him dearly. Scyld Scefing was set adrift, no man knows where. He was found, a tiny child, on the shores of Denmark. But he became a mighty king. All the neighbouring tribes, over the whale's way, had to obey him and pay him tribute.'

'Even the Geats,' added Hygelac in disgust. 'Do you know, we had to pay the Danes tribute? Never again!'

'And when he died,' said Wanderer, 'he returned to the ocean by which he had come. He was laid by the mast, as Balder will be, surrounded by weapons and treasure. They placed a golden banner above his head and let the waves take him, they bequeathed him to the sea.'

In Wanderer's hands, the harp cried the stabbing cries of seabirds, and wept the salt-waves' weeping.

'Scyld's son was Beow and his grandson Healfdene,' said Wanderer, 'both brave kings. But I sing now of Scyld's great-grandson, the living king, Hrothgar.'

Beowulf nodded. Hrothgar! He had known it.

'When he was a young man, Hrothgar built a glorious feasting-hall, the finest on this middle-earth. Heorot. He called it Heorot. Day after day the rafters echoed with the din of merrymaking, men drinking mead and ale. Year after year the king rewarded his followers with gifts at the feast — arm-rings of twisted gold, brooches, buckles, belts, beaver-skin bags, can you imagine it?'

My father has stood on that hall-floor; Hrothgar gave my father treasures in Heorot: that's what Beowulf was thinking.

'And can you imagine,' said Wanderer, pausing and piercing Beowulf with his sword of an eye, 'there was one, just one outsider who could not bear the sounds coming from the hall — the laughter, the happiness, the poet's song and harp in harmony?'

Wanderer spun round, raised his elbows, spread out his cloak, and pointed at his monstrous shadow on the wall, the shadow reaching right above the gables.

'Grendel!' growled Wanderer. 'Grendel is his name.'

The hall was firelit and warm and the Geats there felt chill.

'No one knows where he lives. He ranges the moors, the fen and the fastness. He is the father of every evil being — monsters and dark elves and spiteful spirits.' Wanderer slowly turned back to face his audience. 'One night Grendel came to Heorot, he came calling on the Danes when they were dead drunk, sprawled out and snoring. That monster barged in and broke the necks of thirty thanes. Thirty! He carried them out into the night and away to his lair.'

Beowulf crouched on the edge of a bench, intent, almost angry.

'Next morning,' said Wanderer, 'when Hrothgar came to the hall, its guardians were gone — all thirty of them. And of Grendel there was not a trace except his ... gruesome spoor.' Wanderer said the words so that no one could mistake them, or escape them.

'He was back next day,' continued Wanderer. 'And after that the Danes learned their lesson. Those who had escaped his clutches stowed themselves into dark crannies and corners in the outbuildings. The great hall Heorot stood deserted after nightfall.'

Hygelac shook his head and breathed deeply.

'For twelve years now Grendel has terrorized the Danes. Men and women and children, old and young, they all live under the dark death-shadow. He is so strong, so huge, so loathsome, that no one is able to do anything about it.'

'I will then!' Beowulf leaped up in front of the Geats and heard himself shouting, 'I will then!'

Wanderer's eye gleamed. He watched the warrior, unblinking, and spurred him on.

'All right, Beowulf,' called the king. 'That's as it should be.'

There were cheers in Hygelac's hall.

'You've proved yourself much the strongest man here,' said the king. 'Now prove it elsewhere! Brave men should seek fame in far-off lands.'

The cheers were renewed, there were shouts and boasts in the hall. The mead-horn passed from man to man, and each of them toasted Beowulf.

THE next morning Beowulf chose fourteen men, as keen and well-tempered as warriors can be, to travel with him to Denmark.

The stronghold of the Geats rang with the blows of black-smiths and swung to the shouts of chandlers as armour was made ready and a boat was fitted out for the sea-voyage.

On the third day, there were kisses and embraces on the windswept beach; some said they feared that Beowulf and his companions would never return, some wept, some said nothing.

Then the warriors were eager to begin their journey. They turned their backs on mothers and fathers, on wives and children; they springheeled over the shingle and embarked.

The great sea-bird rode over the breakers. And as soon as the Geats

hoisted a sail, a bleached sea-garment, the boat foamed at the prow and surged over the waves, urged on by the wind.

After that day and the night that darkened it, the warriors sighted shining cliffs, steep headlands – the shores of Denmark.

A Danish coastguard stood on a cliff-top. He watched the boat beat across the black-and-dazzling field of water, and heard it beach screaming on the shingle. When he saw men carrying flashing shields and gleaming war-gear down the gangway, he leaped on his horse, and brandishing a spear, galloped down to the water's edge.

'Warriors!' he shouted. 'Who are you? Where do you come from?'

Beowulf held up his right hand like a flag. 'Peace!'

'Your names!' demanded the coastguard. 'What are you doing here? Before you step one foot further into Denmark.'

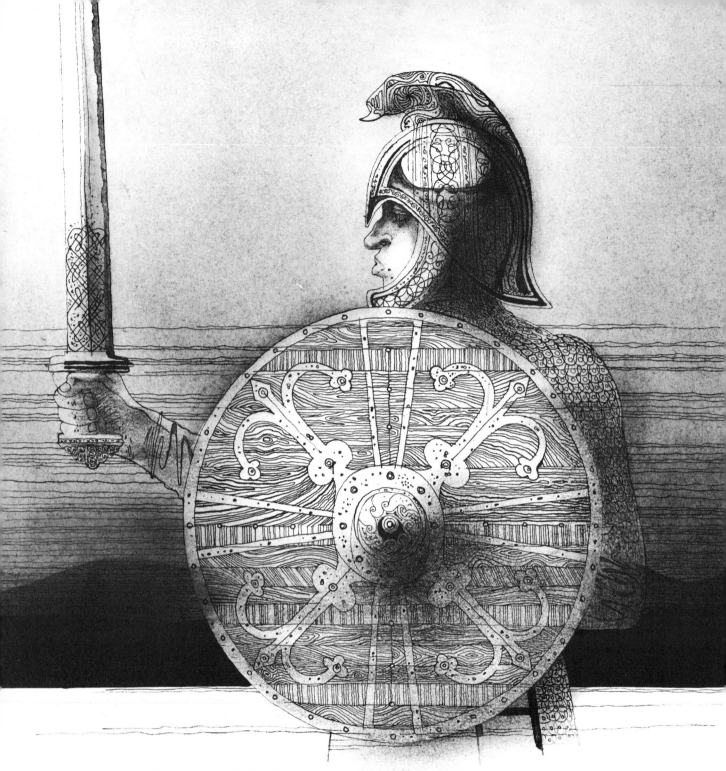

'Friends of the Danes!' called Beowulf.

'Foes of the monster!' said one of his companions.

'That's the sum of it,' Beowulf said. 'We're all Geats. And I am Beowulf, the son of Ecgtheow.

We've heard that Grendel has laid his hand on the Danes.'

'No man can stand against him,' said the coastguard.

'That is why we've come,' said Beowulf. 'I'm here to pit myself - against this monster. I mean to put an end to Grendel.'

A long bright gaze, a slow nod, a half-smile. 'Brave words,' said the coastguard. 'But every wise man knows that a wide ocean divides words from deeds.'

Beowulf smiled and inclined his head.

Then the coastguard welcomed Beowulf and his companions, undertook to watch over their boat, and set them on the paved road that led to Heorot.

In high spirits, the Geats headed for the hall of the Danish king. Their helmets, crowned with boar-crests, shone under the sun; strong links of shining chain-mail clinked together.

They followed the track over the surges of lonely moorland and, before dark, marched up to the huge timbered hall hung with many antlers, hemmed in by outbuildings.

Heorot, Hrothgar's court, bright home of brave men! A muster of warriors hurried out to meet the Geats, and challenged them as the coastguard had done.

'I am Beowulf, and my news is for the king.'

'Have you come as exiles?' asked one Danish warrior.

'Or,' said another man, 'out of ambition?'

'My news is for Hrothgar,' Beowulf repeated. 'You'll hear about it soon enough. Ask him, will he give us leave to speak with him?'

The Danes told Beowulf and his band to leave all their weapons against one wall: linden shields inlaid with gold, coats of mail, a grey-tipped forest of ash-spears. Then they led the Geats into Heorot.

WOVEN stories on the four walls, a gamut of famous men and daring deeds, amber and umber, blue and green and gold; golden mistballs at the candlelit tables; gleaming disks and garnets set into the mead-benches; a waft of herbs, rosemary and thyme; a hundred voices lifted in harmony.

As Beowulf and his companions entered Heorot, and looked round in wonder, the noise fell back in front of them. Watched by curious Danes, they walked up a silent clearing, right up to the king ensconced on his throne.

10

'Greetings, Hrothgar! I am Beowulf the Geat, Ecgtheow's son.'

'Ecgtheow's son?' Hrothgar's kind old face was creased and grey. 'You are welcome then, and so are your companions.'

'Is it true,' Beowulf demanded, 'this hall, even your own hall, is unsafe after dark?'

Hrothgar grimaced. 'Every day at dusk the talking must stop. Drinking must stop. Those still alive have to leave this hall.'

'I,' said Beowulf, 'am thirty strong. I am going to crush this monster in single combat.'

At once the hall began to ripple with excited cross-currents of sound.

Hrothgar gazed at the young warrior, his eyes so full of light; then his own eyes glazed, you could tell he was travelling the green roads of memory. It's because of his father, Hrothgar was thinking; he's come because I once sheltered Ecgtheow, and paid off his feud, isn't that it? The king got up and grasped Beowulf's right hand.

'And I've heard this monster is so reckless he does without weapons,' Beowulf said.

Hrothgar's face crumpled in pain.

'I'll fight on equal terms, then. No sword ...'

'Beowulf ...' objected Hrothgar.

'... and no yellow shield. I'll grapple this fiend hand to hand.' Beowulf paused. 'Hygelac, my king, would expect no less.'

'Beowulf ...' began Hrothgar, but the Geat cut him off a second time:

'And he should have this coat-of-mail if I die. This corslet made by Weland. Send it back to Hygelac.'

'As you ask,' said Hrothgar.

Beowulf shrugged. 'Who knows? Fate goes always as it must.'

'First,' said Hrothgar, putting a hand on Beowulf's arm and turning him round to face the Danish warriors, 'take your place at our feast. Eat and drink after your long journey.'

A bench was cleared for the fifteen Geats. One man brought hunks of boiled pork, and another wholemeal bread; a third carried an arm-cask and an adorned ale-cup, and each of the warriors emptied it in one draught. They stretched and relaxed, their blood began to sing.

The Danes had been drinking all day. Boisterous, brooding, snoring, sitting or sprawling, they surrounded the band of Geats; the king's two sons were amongst them.

One of the Danes, a burly man with beetling eyebrows, glared at Beowulf. 'So,' he called out. 'This Geat, this Geat thinks he can succeed where we failed, does he?'

'Who is that man?' said Beowulf.

'Me,' leered the man. 'I'm Unferth. And I can tell a story about you, Beowulf.'

'Keep it to yourself, Unferth,' said another Dane.

And another, 'You're asking for trouble.'

'Let him tell it!' said Beowulf. 'I'm curious to hear it. Speak up, Unferth.'

'You won't get far with Grendel,' said Unferth. 'Never! Not if you're the same man who went swimming with Breca. I've heard about your contest: who could swim the longer?' Unferth twice banged the table with his fist. 'After seven days you gave up. Breca had you beat.'

'You're drunk, Unferth. I'll tell you the true story. Breca and I swam side by side for five days and five nights, until the tides tore us apart.'

'Big man!' sneered Unferth. 'Tchah!'

'Foaming water! Freezing cold! We each held a naked sword to ward off whales.'

'Whales, eh?' said Unferth unpleasantly. 'Whitebait, more likely.'

'Breca was washed up,' said Beowulf calmly, 'but I was dragged down to the ocean-bed by a sea-monster. I fought with it and buried my sword in its breast.'

Beowulf's companions growled in support.

'If a man is brave enough,' said Beowulf, 'and not doomed to die, fate often spares him to fight another day.'

Unferth rubbed his bloodshot eyes. 'You?' he jeered. 'You're a grinning Geat! A pop … pop … a poppycock hero!'

'And you, Unferth,' said Beowulf, 'who are you to talk.'

Again the Geats growled.

'You cannot bear another man's success. Where others sing praises, you sow dragon's teeth. If your actions matched your big mouth, Grendel would never have caused such havoc in Heorot.'

Unferth spat on the ground and said nothing.

'Grendel does as he likes with Danes, but soon, very soon, I'll show this monster what the Geats are made of.'

With that, Beowulf turned his back on Unferth and, as he did so, he saw the Danish queen, Wealhtheow, entering the hall: purple gown, and long grey hair, and violet eyes.

Flanked by two ladies-in-waiting, Wealhtheow swept up to the dais, and there the ale-thane put the adorned cup into her hands. The queen offered it first to the king, and then she walked over to Beowulf and offered it next to him.

'Lady!' Beowulf said, 'I have come to deliver your people or die in Grendel's clutches. That is my choice. Here, in this hall, I'll kill this monster or lay down my life.'

'Twelve winters without hope,' said Wealhtheow slowly.

She paused and smiled sadly at the Geat. 'At least we have hope tonight.'

'Since it was built,' called Hrothgar, 'this great hall Heorot has never been guarded by anyone but Danes. Take it, look after it! Give no quarter, Beowulf!'

Then all the Danish warriors rose from their seats and, led by Hrothgar and his queen, made their way out of the hall and into the gathering dark, away to the safety of the outbuildings.

There was almost silence in Heorot.

The Geats looked round, they listened to the hall creak in the small nightwind, and they began to lay aside their helmets and corslets.

Then each man took a bolster from one corner of the hall and found himself a sleeping-place.

'Leave him to me!' said Beowulf. 'I'll fight him hand to hand.'

The Geats lay down and spoke in low voices. Except for Beowulf, not one of them believed he would see the next day or dawn, or ever go back to his family and friends.

THROUGH the dark night a darker shape slid. A sinister figure shrithed down from the moors, over high shoulders, sopping tussocks, over sheep-runs, over gurgling streams. It shrithed towards the timbered hall, huge and hairy and slightly stooping. Its long arms swung loosely.

One man was snoring, one mumbling, one coughing; all the Geats guarding Heorot had fallen asleep – all except one, one man watching.

For a moment the shape waited outside the hall. It cocked an ear. It began to quiver. Its hair bristled. Then it grasped the great ring-handle and swung open the door, the mouth of Heorot. It lunged out of the darkness and into the circle of dim candleight, it took a long stride across the patterned floor.

Through half-closed eyes Beowulf was watching, and through barred teeth he breathed one word. 'Grendel.' The name of the monster, the loathsome syllables.

Grendel saw the knot of sleeping warriors and his eyes shone with an unearthly light. He lurched towards the nearest man, a brave Geat called Leofric, scooped him up and, with one ghastly claw, choked the scream in his throat. Then the monster ripped him apart, bit into his body, drank the blood from his veins, devoured huge pieces; within one minute he had swallowed the whole man, even his feet and hands.

Still the Geats slept. The air in Heorot was thick with their sleep, thicker still with death and the stench of the monster.

Grendel slobbered spittle and blood; his first taste of flesh only made him more ravenous. He wheeled round towards Beowulf, stooped, reached out for him, and Beowulf ...

Beowulf leaped up and stayed the monster's outstretched arm.

Grendel grunted and pulled back. And at that sound, all the other Geats were instantly awake. They grabbed their swords, they backed off, they shouted for Beowulf.

Grendel tried to break free but Beowulf held him fast. The monster snorted and tugged, he could feel his fingers cracking in the Geat's grip.

Now the great room boomed. Clang and clatter shattered the night-silence as Beowulf and Grendel lurched to and fro in their deathly tug-of-war. Tables and mead-benches were overturned, Grendel roared and snarled, and in the outbuildings Danes woke and listened in the darkness.

When the Geats saw that Grendel could not escape Beowulf's grip, they surrounded him and slashed at him with their swords.

Heorot flashed with battle-lights. Those warriors did not know that no kind of weapon, not even the finest iron on earth, could wound their enemy. His skin was like old rind, tough and almost hard; he had woven a secret spell against every kind of battle-blade.

Now Beowulf twisted Grendel's right arm behind his neck. He locked it and turned it, slowly he turned it, putting terrible pressure on Grendel's shoulder.

The monster bellowed and dropped to one knee. He jerked and his whole body shuddered and trembled. With superhuman strength he jerked again as he tried to escape Beowulf's grip, he jerked and all at once, his right shoulder ripped. A ghastly tearing of muscle and sinew and flesh; a spurting of hot blood: the monster's arm came apart from his body. Grendel howled. He staggered away from Beowulf, and reeled out of the hall.

The Geats cheered and shouted; they hugged one another; they converged on Beowulf.

Beowulf was gasping. 'I wanted to throttle him ...'

'He's finished!' roared one Geat.

'... here and now.'

'Done for!' shouted another.

'I couldn't hold him ... not strong enough ...'

'Wherever he goes,' said a third companion, 'death goes with him.'

'I've done as I said,' Beowulf panted, 'and avenged Leofric.'

Until that very moment, the Geats were not aware that they had lost one of their companions. They listened as Beowulf told them what had happened when Grendel first came to the hall; and all their joy at the monster's death turned to anger and gloom at the fate of Leofric.

'Look at this hand!' muttered one man.

'Each nail like steel.'

'Each claw, I'd say.'

'Ten terrifying spikes.'

'Hand, arm and shoulder.'

'No man can withstand Beowulf . . .'

'. . . and no monster neither.'

Beowulf raised a hand and the Geats fell silent.

'Hang it up!' Beowulf said. 'Stick it up outside the door, under the gable. And then give Hrothgar news of my victory.'

Beowulf's companions hastened to do as he asked. One man climbed onto another's shoulders just outside the great door, and by guttering candlelight secured Grendel's grasp, bloodstained and battle-hardened, under the gable. Two others found brands at the hearth, rekindled them in the embers, and headed for the outbuildings.

Within a few minutes the first Danish warriors hurried into the hall. Others followed on their heels and then, at dawn, as the eastern sky turned pale green mackerel, the king himself proceeded to the hall on his old unsteady legs, supported by Wealhtheow, his queen. He paused at the door, marvelled at the monster's grasp, and then embraced Beowulf.

'This hall Heorot,' Beowulf said, 'I return it to you. Once again you can call it your own.'

'I'd lost hope,' Hrothgar said. 'Lost all belief that anyone could end it, this monstrous nightmare.'

'Twelve winters,' said Wealhtheow.

'I kept my word,' Beowulf said, 'and fought hand to hand on equal terms.'

'Beowulf, best of men, from this day on I will treat you like a son; whatever I have here on this middle-earth will be yours also.'

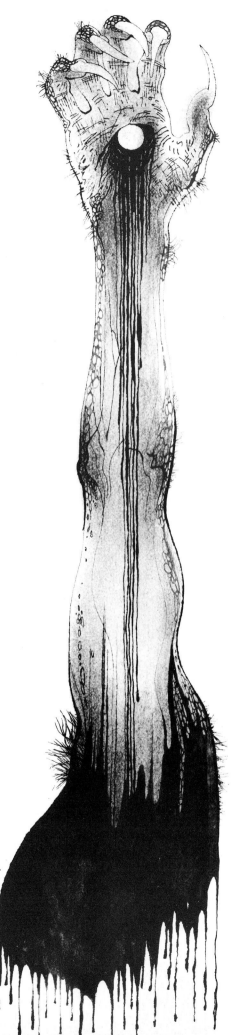

21

Wealhtheow looked troubled at the king's words, but she smiled and said nothing. Once more Hrothgar stepped forward and embraced Beowulf.

Word of Grendel's death quickly spread far and wide. Throughout that day hundreds of Danes converged on Heorot to stare at the monster's cruel grasp, and in the evening Hrothgar held a feast in honour of Beowulf and the Geats.

The king gave Beowulf shining rewards for killing Grendel – a stiff battle banner woven with gold thread, a helmet incised with battle scenes, a coat-of-mail and, finest of all, the huge damascened sword that once belonged to Healfdene, the king's own father.

Then, at a sign from Hrothgar, eight horses with gold-plated bridles pranced into the hall. 'This saddle,' said Hrothgar, 'so well cut and inlaid with precious stones, this is my own. Take it and take these horses, and make good use of them.'

Finally, Hrothgar gave a gold buckle to each of the Geats who had crossed the sea with Beowulf, and decreed that gold should be paid for the life of the warrior Leofric.

The warriors drank and feasted and drank again. Then the poet sang a lay, he compared Beowulf to Sigemund, the dragon-slayer. Waves of noise broke out along the benches, talk and laughter.

'As it used to be,' said Hrothgar.

'And will be,' said Wealhtheow. 'Give rewards, Hrothgar, while you may. But remember your own sons! Leave this land, leave this Danish people to our sons when the day comes for you to die.'

At the end of the evening, Hrothgar and Wealhtheow retired to their quarters, and Beowulf was conducted to a bed in the outbuildings where he could sleep alone and more peacefully; he was weary after his night's work. But all the other Danes and Geats remained in Heorot.

Benches were pushed back, the whole floor was padded with bolsters and pillows; and at each man's head, his helmet and coat-of-mail, his spear and shield, gleamed in the gloom.

Silence in the hall, dark and deeper dark, another night for men: one of the feasters sleeping in Heorot was doomed and soon to die …

I N the middle of the night, two servants with flaming torches roused Beowulf from his sleep and escorted him to Hrothgar's chamber.

'Aeschere!' said the king. He shook his head and his face creased, a grey grief-map. 'Now Aeschere!'

'I am here,' Beowulf said.

'Aeschere is dead. My dear old friend, my battle companion.'

'In the hall?'

'Two monsters! Just as some men have said, there are two monsters after all, rulers of the moors, rangers of the fell-country. Grendel and his mother, and it will never end.'

'It will end,' Beowulf said.

'She came to Heorot,' said the king. 'She barged into the hall, mournful and ravenous, snatched down Grendel's grasp from the gable, seized the nearest man – Aeschere! My friend!'

'Vengeance,' Beowulf said.

'She just tucked him under her arm, and made off into the darkness.'

'There is honour amongst monsters as there is honour amongst men. Grendel's mother came to the hall to avenge the death of her son.'

'Once again, Beowulf, help may be had from you alone.'

'Do not grieve,' Beowulf said.

'Her lair is away and over the misty moors, at the bottom of a lake.'

'Better each man should avenge his dead, as Grendel's mother has done. Your days are numbered and my days are numbered …'

Beowulf put a hand on the old king's arm. 'He who can should win renown, fame before death. That is a warrior's best memorial in this world. I promise you, Hrothgar, that wherever she turns – honeycomb caves, mountain woods – I will hunt her down.'

As soon as night eased, Beowulf's stallion, one of Hrothgar's gifts, was saddled and bridled. He left Heorot at once, accompanied by the king, his own companions and a large group of Danes.

They followed the monster's tracks through the forest and over the hills. Then they headed into little-known country, wolf-slopes, windswept headlands, perilous ways across boggy moors. They waded through a freezing stream that plunged from beetling crags and rushed seething through a fissure, picked their way along string-thin paths, skirted small

lakes where water-demons lived; at last they came to a dismal wood, stiff with hoar-frost, standing on the edge of a precipice.

The lake lay beneath, the lair of Grendel and his gruesome mother. It was blood-stained and troubled. Whipped waves reared up and reached for the sky until the air was misty, and heaven weeped.

The Geats and Danes made their way down to the side of the water. Beowulf braced his shoulders, put on his clinking corslet, and donned his

helmet hung with chain-mail to guard his neck. Then Unferth stepped forward.

Beowulf looked at him coldly; he had not forgotten their encounter in the hall.

'I did you a great wrong in Heorot,' Unferth said. 'Too much beer.'

'What's past is past,' Beowulf said.

'You're the only man alive who would risk this fight.'

'Then it's right I should risk it.'

'Take my sword, Beowulf. Hrunting! It never fails.'

Beowulf grasped the sword, smiled and clapped Unferth on the shoulder. Then he turned to Hrothgar. 'If this monster covers me with a sheet of shining blood ...'

'No, Beowulf!'

'... then look after my companions. Send my gifts to Hygelac. And give this great sword back to Unferth.'

Beowulf did not even wait for an answer. He dived from the bank into the water, and one of the Geats put a horn to his lips and blew an eager battle-song.

For a whole day Beowulf stroked down through the water. Then Grendel's mother saw him heading for her lair; the sea-wolf rose to meet

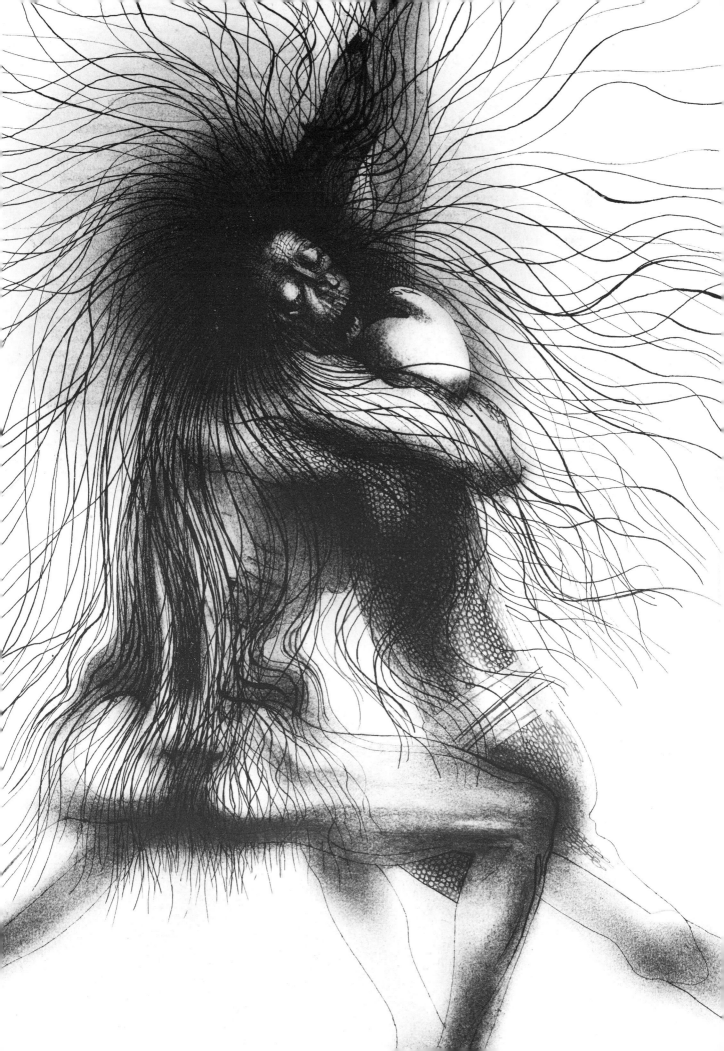

him, clutched at him, grabbed him, swept him down and into a great vaulted chamber, a hall underwater, untouched by water.

The Geat wrestled free of Grendel's mother; she was coated with her own filth, red-eyed and roaring. He whirled the sword Hrunting, and played terrible war-music on the monster's skull. Grendel's mother roared the louder but Beowulf saw she was unharmed.

'Useless!' he shouted. 'It's useless! Or else magic spells protect her.' He hurled the sword away and began to grapple with Grendel's mother.

Beowulf threw the monster to the ground. But then she tripped him, held him in a fearsome clinch and drew a dagger. Beowulf could not throw her off. Then Grendel's mother stabbed at Beowulf's heart. She stabbed again. But the cunning links of chain-mail held firm and guarded Beowulf; his corslet saved him.

Now the Geat sprang to his feet. He saw a sword, massive and double-edged, made by giants, lying in one corner of the chamber. It was so huge that only he of all men could have handled it.

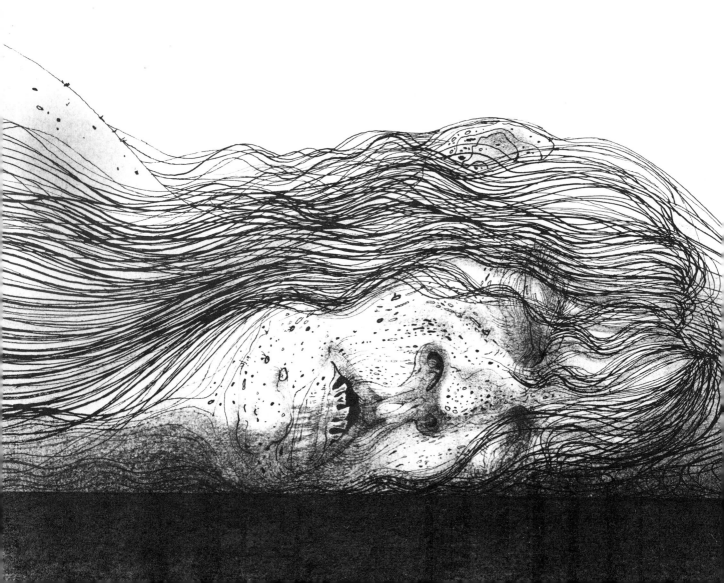

Beowulf ran across the floor, gripped the ringed hilt and swung the ornamented sword – he struck Grendel's mother as she lumbered towards him. The blade slashed through her neck, smashed the vertebrae. The monster moaned and fell dead at his feet.

For a long while Beowulf leaned on the blood-stained sword; his heart was pounding. A man with the strength of thirty! Slayer of Grendel and slayer of the sea-wolf! A hero without equal in this middle-world!

Then Beowulf looked about him. He saw a recess, a small cave, and in the cave he found Grendel's body, drained of life-blood. 'As a trophy,' Beowulf said grimly and, with one blow, he severed the monster's head. 'Your head and this massive sword.'

The Geat spoke too soon. The patterned blade had begun to drip and melt like a gory icicle. Because of the venom in the monster's blood, it thawed entirely, right up to the hilt. So Beowulf grasped all that remained of it, picked up the sword Hrunting and Grendel's head, and left that vaulted chamber. He swam up through the water.

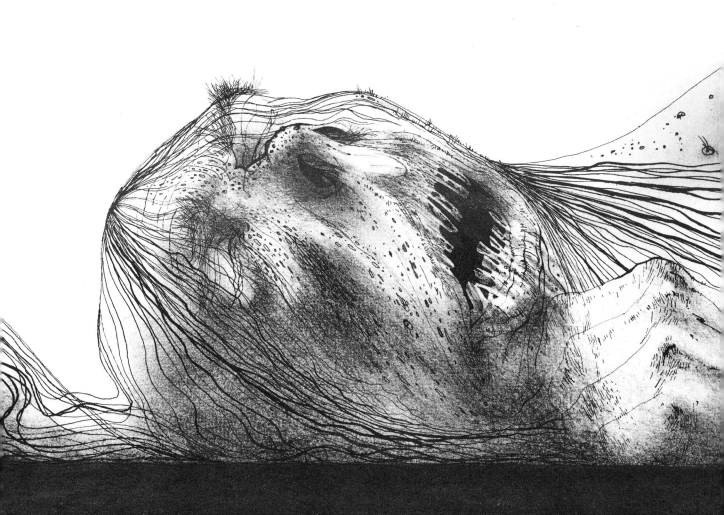

Beowulf's companions, still waiting at the lakeside, were overjoyed to see their leader. They handed him up on to the bank and marvelled at his trophies. Quickly they relieved him of his helmet and corslet.

'After the ninth hour,' one Geat said, 'it seemed hopeless.'

'We still hoped,' said another.

'And the Danes?' Beowulf asked.

'They went back to Heorot,' said one man.

And another: 'When the water boiled with blood, they thought it was all over.'

'So it was,' said Beowulf. 'For Grendel's mother!'

The Geats tied Grendel's head to a great pole, a battering-ram; four of them shouldered it. Then with songs on their lips, Beowulf and his companions left the lake. The journey back to the gold-hall seemed far shorter than their outward journey, and that same evening they carried the monster's head onto the floor where the warriors were drinking – a ghastly sight paraded before Hrothgar and his queen.

Beowulf walked up before the gift-throne, firm-footed, flanked by his companions. 'Hrothgar,' he said, 'son of Healfdene, ruler of the Danes! Proudly we lay before you plunder from the lake!'

Hrothgar shook his white head and smiled and embraced the Geat. 'Beowulf,' he said, 'bravest of men, fate's darling! Your friends are fortunate, your enemies not to be envied!'

'Even Hrunting was useless,' said Beowulf. 'But it was my ally; do not think I underrate it.' He returned the sword to Unferth and thanked him for the loan of it.

'Tell us all and everything,' urged the old king.

'I tell you, Hrothgar, you and your warriors can sleep in this gold-hall without fear. The death-shadow will skulk near Heorot no longer.'

Then Beowulf related what had happened after he had left the Geats and Danes at the lakeside. The companions ate and drank and, weary in their bones, lay down to rest.

The great hall Heorot soared, spacious and adorned with gold; the guests slept within until the black raven proclaimed sunrise. Bright lights chased away the shadows of the night.

In the morning, Geats and Danes met in the hall once again, and

Beowulf told Hrothgar that, now that Grendel and his mother were dead, he and his companions were eager to return home.

'Stay a little longer,' Hrothgar said. 'Will you stay?'

'No man could have treated us with greater kindness. But I must tell Hygelac ... we want to see our families and friends.'

'Your people,' said the king, 'would do well to choose you as Hygelac's successor. They could not have a better king.'

'If ever you need me,' Beowulf said, 'send for me and I will come. I'll come at once, ready for combat, and bring warriors by the thousand ...' 'And because of your exploits, the old enmity between Geats and Danes will come to an end,' Hrothgar said, his voice rising.

Beowulf took the arm of the old king.

'For as long as I live,' Hrothgar continued, 'Geats and Danes will exchange treasures; men will send gifts over the seas where gannets swoop and rise.'

Then Hrothgar gave Beowulf twelve great treasures, and kissed and embraced him; tears streamed down the king's face. He was old and knew he was unlikely ever to see brave Beowulf again. He couldn't conceal his sense of loss; in his heart and in his head, in his very blood, a deep love burned for that young warrior.

So Beowulf and the Geats bade farewell to Hrothgar, Wealhtheow, and the Danish warriors. They left the gold-hall Heorot, taking all their treasure with them. On their stallions they galloped over the empty moorland. They hurried towards their waiting boat and the rocking sea, the gulls' path, the whale-road to their own dear country.

AFTER Hygelac had died, and his son was killed in battle, Beowulf ruled the Geats for fifty years. Seasons of peace, once Beowulf had beaten off the grasping Swedes, murderous Frisians, cruel Franks; seasons of friendship, as Hrothgar had foretold, between Geats and Danes. Old Beowulf was a strong land-guardian, a wise king.

From Beowulf's hall and the buildings clustered around it – the stronghold of the Geats – a windswept moor reached up to the headland of Eagleness. That was a desolate place, a prow of land jutting out into the ocean, precipitous, riddled with caves.

One night a slave on the run, a poor man who preferred the misery of exile to his master's whip, took refuge in one of these caves. At dawn the slave stiffened in horror. He saw there was a dragon in that cave. A serpent, scaled and sleeping! And all around the dragon lay a shining hoard: precious stones, silver, gold; goblets, plates and vessels, rings. It had guarded that treasure for three hundred winters.

The slave was terrified. He lifted the nearest piece, a gold goblet, picked his way right past the dragon's head and out of the cave, and hared over the moor towards Beowulf's hall.

When the dragon woke from its long sleep, it realized at once that its hoard had been robbed: it snorted and a twisting flame-torque leaped out of its mouth. The dragon took revenge. As soon as it was dark it swooped on the Geats and girdled their stronghold with fire.

When day dawned once more, Beowulf and his companions saw the terrible damage and destruction – buildings gutted or collapsed, exposed to the elements; charred gables and beams; smouldering heaps of ash. All the land round about had been laid waste; it looked like fields of stubble fired after harvesting.

Beowulf called the warrior Geats to a meeting. They gathered in the hall of his young cousin Wiglaf; it was made of stone, the only place in the stronghold to have escaped the fire.

A crowd of pale faces; a current of voices; a counting of heads.

'Never,' said Beowulf, 'has there been an enemy such as this. But if we wait, it will be worse: this dragon will pay us a second visit.'

The men around him listened and said nothing.

'There's only one way to put an end to this threat, and only one man who can do it.'

'We've sworn oaths,' protested young Wiglaf. 'I'll never have it said ...'

'You've never fought in single combat,' Beowulf interrupted. 'I wrenched off Grendel's arm; I killed his mother.'

'Fifty years, Beowulf.'

'I know myself, cousin Wiglaf. Old I may be, but I'll fight this fight alone.'

Wiglaf shook his head unhappily.

'A linden shield will be no use. As soon as this weapon-smith has forged a shield of iron, I'll head for Eagleness.'

'At least let some of us come with you,' said Wiglaf.

'As you like. I'll need that wretched thief to show me the way.'

Later that day, Beowulf and eleven Geats, grim-faced in their helmets, left the smoking stronghold and made their way up on to Eagleness. Much against his will, the slave led them to the entrance to the dragon's cave perched high above the ocean, the fretting water.

Beowulf sat on the headland. His mind was mournful, angry for slaughter. 'This is not your fight,' he said to his companions, 'you, loyal Wiglaf, or any of you. I'll kill this dragon and win the gold-hoard for the Geats, or ... This life is very short, but not the fame, the good name that live after it.'

Then Beowulf walked up under the cliff and saw steaming water spurting through a stone arch – the entrance to the cave. The leader of the Geats felt battle-anger begin to pump inside him. He threw out his chest and gave a great roar; he hammered the grey rock's anvil.

At once a guff of smoke issued from the cave; the cliff itself snarled. As the dragon slithered down the slope towards him, Beowulf brandished his sword Naegling. He slashed at the serpent's neck, but he could not pierce its scale-corslet. Flames leaped through the air, brighter than day's bright light; Beowulf sheltered behind his shield.

'This is no fight for us,' said one Geat. 'He was right.'

'No place for us neither.'

'One lick of that fire and we'll all be cinders.'

Wiglaf angrily rounded on his companions. 'Beowulf gave us rings, armour, helmets, tempered swords: we all swore to help him if ever the need arose.'

'You heard him,' said one man. 'You heard what Beowulf said.'

'We'd do best to save our own lives.'

'You rat!' shouted Wiglaf. He turned his back on his cowardly companions and stormed up the slope towards Beowulf, calling, 'Fight for your name! Fight for your fame! I'm here and I'll help you.'

The dragon welcomed Wiglaf with a blast of flame that set fire to his shield. The young warrior sweltered and crouched behind Beowulf's huge iron shield.

As the dragon wheeled, dragging its monstrous body over the scree, Beowulf stood up and crashed Naegling against its head. The sword point stuck in its skull! Then the serpent writhed and bucked and Naegling was not strong enough; it bent and it snapped.

Beowulf stared in dismay at his old grey-hued sword and at once the dragon lunged forward. It gripped Beowulf's neck between its sharp teeth. The old king was bathed in blood; it poured out of his arteries and veins.

Quickly Wiglaf took three strides and sank his sword into the dragon's belly. He buried it up to the hilt. The dragon gasped, and let go of Beowulf's neck, and at once the flames began to abate.

Then Beowulf fumbled for the deadly knife fastened to his corslet. He closed his eyes and swayed, then he launched himself forward, fell against the dragon and slit its throat.

The serpent gargled. It jerked and shuddered; it lay still.

Beowulf's neck-wound began to burn and swell; the dragon's poison gave him great pain. He tottered forward and slumped on a ledge.

Wiglaf unfastened the old king's helmet; then as Beowulf asked, he hurried up to the cave and brought out some of the hoard so that Beowulf could see it before he died.

'A gold cup,' he said. 'This salver ... this banner made of nothing but gold thread. There are weapons in there too, enough for an army. I could not carry them.'

'Now this great hoard belongs to the Geats,' Beowulf said. 'And you, cousin Wiglaf, in days to come you must lead and serve our people.'

Wiglaf came close to the old king for his voice was failing; he could only whisper.

'After the funeral fire, ask the warriors to build a barrow overlooking the sea.'

'It will be,' said Wiglaf.

'Let it tower high on Whaleness . . . Beowulf's barrow . . . a beacon for seafarers.'

'It will be so.'

Beowulf gave his golden collar to Wiglaf, his helmet, ring, and corslet. 'Take them, Wiglaf. You're the last survivor of our family. The rest are dead, and I must follow them.'

Beowulf almost smiled, he sighed and closed his eyes. Wiglaf looked at him tenderly and tears sprang to his eyes. He stared at his lord and he stared at the prostrate dragon, both of them swept away by fate.

For a while Wiglaf sat beside the body of his king, thinking of time past, and time to come. He did not hear his cowardly companions until there were sighs at his shoulder, sorrowful looks, cringing words.

'Ten oath-breakers,' said Wiglaf coldly. 'Where did you come from? Where did you slink up from?'

'Wiglaf . . .'

'When men hear about you, they'll condemn you to exile – far from your families, far from your own land. You've forfeited forever the happiness of home.' Wiglaf would have nothing of their protests and excuses. 'I tell you, death would be better than your disgrace.'

Then the young warrior told the slave to hurry down to the stronghold, and give the news of Beowulf's death to the waiting warriors.

Later that day, a great crowd of Geats set out for Eagleness. They mourned over the body of the old king. And they marvelled at the loathsome dragon, its scales burnished orange and brown and green, its coils and folded wings, its forked tongue. One man measured it: fifty paces from head to tail. They pushed that serpent over the precipice; they gave him to the dark waves far beneath, the heaving waters.

Then, led by Wiglaf, the Geats swarmed into the dragon's cave and reaped the gold-harvest – goblets and vessels of solid gold, salvers,

precious swords – and carried it back with Beowulf's body to the scorched stronghold.

'The Swedes,' said Wiglaf, 'and the Frisians and the Franks have been waiting for this: the day when our lord laid aside laughter, festivity, happiness.' The young warrior was weary in spirit and body. 'Soon enough our hands will hold many a spear chill with dawn-cold. The dark raven will tell the eagle of the feast when, with the wolf, it laid bare the bones of corpses.'

In the morning, every man carried one faggot up to Whaleness. And there the Geats built a funeral pyre, hung round with helmets and shields and shining mail. Then they brought Beowulf's body from the stronghold on a waggon and placed it on the pyre.

'Farewell to our king,' Wiglaf called out over the sound of weeping, the voices of wind and fire, 'who often braved the iron-tipped arrow-shower. The man who killed a monster and his monstrous mother! Dragon-slayer!'

The Geats all mourned the death of their king; a maiden sang a dirge dark with dread of days to come; and a man with one gleaming eye walked amongst them, saying, 'It is finished. Now it is finished. And you finished it.'

The dark wood-smoke soared over the fire; Beowulf's body became ash, consumed to its core. Sky swallowed the plume.

It took the Geats ten days to build Beowulf's barrow, a great beacon known throughout the north world. At its heart lay Beowulf's ashes. And in his honour, the Geats buried rings and brooches and cups and salvers in that barrow, all the gold Beowulf had gained from the dragon. They bequeathed every piece of shining gold to the earth and there it still remains, untouched by men, of no more use than it was before.

Then twelve warriors rode round the barrow, grave guardians, brave Geats. They chanted a death-song, they talked as men should about their dead and living king. Round and round. They praised his daring deeds, warm words for a breathing name. Round. They said that of all kings on earth, he was the kindest, the most gentle, the most just to his people, the most eager for fame.

Oxford University Press, Walton Street, Oxford OX2 6DP

London Glasgow New York Toronto
Delhi Bombay Calcutta Madras Karachi
Nairobi Dar es Salaam Cape Town Salisbury
Kuala Lumpur Singapore Hong Kong Tokyo
Melbourne Auckland

and associate companies in
Beirut Berlin Ibadan Mexico City Nicosia

Text © Kevin Crossley-Holland 1982
Illustrations © Charles Keeping 1982

British Library Cataloguing in Publication Data
Beowulf.
I. Crossley-Holland, Kevin II. Keeping, Charles
823'.914 [J] PZ7
ISBN 0-19-279770-0

Phototypeset by Tradespools Limited, Frome, Somerset
Printed in Great Britain by Fakenham Press